The Skinwalker Series

In the magical middle ages, humans and Skinwalkers lived side by side. The humans had only one skin, but Skinwalkers could change from human to animal form. This difference led to problems on both sides.

Legend of the Ring *by* D.M. OUELLET Only a stable boy can head off an all-out war between humans and Skinwalkers.

Walking Both Sides *by* C.A. RAINFIELD A teenage boy shoots a Skinwalker, and soon the clans want revenge. Can a teenage girl bring peace between humans and Skinwalkers?

Wolves at the Gate *by* E.L. THOMAS A young pickpocket must flee to the huts of the Skinwalkers to avoid the King's soldiers. But that is only the beginning of his problems.

The SKINWALKER Novels

Legend of the Ring

D.M. OUELLET

LIBRARY AND ARCHIVES CANADA CATALOGUING IN PUBLICATION

Ouellet, Debbie
    Legend of the ring / Debbie Ouellet.

(HIP fantasy)
(Skinwalker novels)
ISBN 978-1-926847-14-6

I. Title. II. Series: HIP fantasy III. Series: Skinwalker novels

PS8629.U33L43 2011   jC813'.6   C2011-900525-5

General editor: Paul Kropp
Text design: Laura Brady
Illustrations drawn by: Charlie Hnatiuk
Cover design: Robert Corrigan

1 2 3 4 5 6 7   15 14 13 12 11

Printed and bound in Canada by Webcom

High Interest Publishing acknowledges the financial support of the Government of Canada through the Canada Book Fund for our publishing activities.

CONTENTS

To Alex and Sarah with love

Prologue

At the dawn of the first forest, clans of Skinwalkers and One-Skins lived side by side. Sometimes the Skinwalkers walked in their animal skins. Sometimes they walked in their human skins. One-Skins — the humans — were their friends.

But that was long ago. Over time, the One-Skins became more powerful. Some thought that Skinwalkers were evil. Some told stories of Skinwalker magic. Then soldiers began to hunt and kill Skinwalkers. Now the few remaining clans must live in hiding.

But all that is about to change. A secret Skinwalker — Lord Damon — seeks revenge against the One-Skins. He plans to unite the Skinwalker clans and wage war against the humans.

The only thing that stands in his way is a stable boy. An orphan. A teenager who does not really know his own powers.

CHAPTER ONE | Wolves!

Wolves must have done this!

Ross bent low. He ran his hand across the dead stallion's still warm body. *How could wolves bring down this giant of a horse?* Ross wondered.

Ross checked the deep, red bites on its throat. He shook his head and frowned. What kind of wolf would sneak into a village and attack in broad daylight? The wolves hadn't even fed on their kill. It didn't make sense. Wolves don't hunt for sport. And this horse wasn't the first. It was the fourth wolf attack in as many days.

"Useless boy!" his uncle barked. "Get a move on and set those wolf traps. Horses cost money. I won't lose another stallion to those wolves."

Ross flinched at the sting of Uncle's words. He should be used to his uncle's cruelty by now, but the old man's words still felt like a knife in the heart. His uncle was the only family Ross had left. But Uncle Axel treated him more like a servant than a nephew.

Ross slung the wolf traps over his shoulder. He kept his eyes to the ground as he headed towards the harbor. Villagers stopped to stare at him as he walked through town. They always did. "His skin's as white as death," he heard one man whisper. "His hair is as red as hell's fire," said another. Many spat on the ground as Ross passed.

Ross gritted his teeth and tried to ignore them. Just like he always did. He kept his eyes low all the way to the harbor.

Ross stopped at the sound of a gruff voice. "Look up, Carrot Head! It's a grand day. You can't see the sun if you don't look for it."

A grin spread across Ross's face at the sound of Bernard's voice. If anyone else had called him Carrot Head, Ross would have bloodied his nose. But Bernard was his friend. His only real friend in the village of Land's End.

Ross waited as Bernard put away his nets from a long day spent fishing. Like Ross, Bernard had just had his sixteenth birthday. But Bernard was big as a bear and twice as clumsy. He cursed as he untangled the net's ropes with huge rough hands. They made a fine pair. Ross was a thin, white-skinned, red-haired orphan. Bernard was the hulking son of a fisherman.

Bernard slapped Ross's back so hard that his teeth shook. "Day's almost at its end. We better get going if we want to make the woods before dark." He lifted the traps from Ross's shoulders as if they were feathers. "Pa says to be extra careful tonight. Folks saw a great black beast in the woods. Twice the size of a wolf, he says."

Soon they had reached the woods that ringed Land's End. Ross was silent as they worked to set the wolf traps. Another sleepless night was taking its toll. Ross had too many sleepless nights lately. Strange and violent dreams kept him awake. Images from the dreams flitted around his mind, but made no sense.

Ross ran a tired hand through his unruly hair, then realized that Bernard was calling his name.

Bernard took Ross by the shoulders. "Where was that carrot brain of yours? I called your name three times." He forced Ross to make eye contact. "What's wrong, Ross? Half the time, you walk around in a daze. You look like you haven't slept in a week."

Of course I don't sleep, thought Ross. *My dreams haunt me. My dead mother's face. The ring she gave me with its strange writing. The words she screamed as the King's guards dragged her away. How can I explain something that I don't understand myself?*

"I'm having those strange dreams again," Ross told his friend. Then he paused as he searched for the right words. "And when I wake up, I feel like I don't belong in my own skin."

Bernard nodded. "My Pa says you should pay attention

to your dreams. They tell you things about yourself."

"Do you believe that?"

"Me? I don't believe much of anything," replied Bernard. "But Pa believes. And Pa's advice is something you can count on."

"So what would your father tell me to do?"

Bernard scratched his chin for a moment. "He'd say to listen to what your dreams are trying to tell you. Then follow where they lead."

Ross stared off into the purple sky and nodded. *My dreams are all about death*, he thought. *If I follow them, let's hope I don't end up as dead as the rest of my family.*

The sun had fully set by the time they rigged the last trap. Then the two friends gathered their gear in silence. Bernard led the way to the trail back to Land's End.

Around them was the darkness of a ghostly night. Mist snaked along the ground. Owls hooted above them. Ross leaned forward with his torch and tried to peer ahead, but he could see nothing. Ross felt the pounding of the horse's hooves long before he heard them. They beat in rhythm with the racing of his heart.

"Someone's coming," he whispered.

"Shhh," Bernard replied.

Howls and whinnies echoed through the mist. Some inner voice told Ross to hide. He found a fallen oak and crouched behind it. Bernard wasn't far behind.

It was none too soon.

A strange girl came racing out of the mist. She had long hair, dark eyes, and a face full of terror. A scream ripped from her throat, startling bats nesting in the trees. "What in the name of . . . ?" Bernard whispered.

A horse followed behind the girl. On its back sat a man dressed in black. The man's pale face reflected the moonlight. White hair streamed from his black hood. He growled deep in his throat and called out, "Stop, thief!" Behind the horseman, running just as fast, were a dozen wolves.

It's Lord Damon! Ross thought. He had heard the stories about Lord Damon but never seen him this close before. No wonder the villagers were so afraid of him. No wonder they called him the Dark Lord.

Ross could imagine what might happen to the girl if Lord Damon caught her. The Dark Lord might force himself upon her, or let the wolves rip her to pieces.

Ross dropped his gear. Bernard held him by the arm before he could bolt from their hiding spot.

"Where are you going?"

"Where do think?" Ross pulled his arm free. "I'm going to save the girl."

CHAPTER TWO | Help Me!

Ross raced through the mist. His legs pumped. His heart pounded wildly. Ross pulled in great gulps of cool night air and put on more speed. *Thump, thump, thump.* His feet beat against the ground. Ross always felt the most alive when he ran.

Somewhere far behind, Bernard called out for him to wait.

Ross grinned in the darkness and ran faster. He followed the howls and yelps. Ross locked onto the sound of beating hooves. His heartbeat matched their rhythm.

Ross wasn't ready when one giant wolf stopped and turned to face him. The wolf stood in the mist, its teeth bared. Its ears were drawn back as it growled.

He only had seconds to make his decision. Should he turn back or try to run past? Could Ross outrun a wolf? The wolf snapped and snarled almost as if it was daring him to do something stupid.

Ross swerved to the left. He planned to cut through the woods and meet up with the trail a hundred yards ahead. An inner voice warned him that the wolf in the road hadn't moved.

Something was wrong.

Then a second wolf leapt from behind a tree. It curled back its upper lip and growled low in its throat.

Ross knew how to change course quickly to avoid a trap. He bolted to the right and cut across the trail to the other side.

A third wolf stepped slowly from behind a bush.

A trap! The wolves had set a trap. How was that possible?

The third wolf yipped and yowled. It sounded strangely like a human laugh.

Instinct made the hairs on Ross's neck stand up. He shifted nervously from one foot to the other. *Stupid. Stupid. Stupid*, he thought. *What am I going to do now?*

Just as he thought he was done for, Ross heard a gruff voice from behind him.

"I told you to wait," Bernard panted, out of breath. Then he thrust forward a flaming torch. "Get out of here, you devils," he shouted.

There's nothing wolves fear more than fire. The three wolves yipped and yelped. Then they bolted back into the darkness of the forest.

Bernard turned to glare at Ross in the torch's light. His friend was still huffing and puffing from his run.

"The next time you decide to race into sure death, make sure you have someone to watch your back," Bernard said.

"It seems I already do." Ross grinned at his friend. "Come then. Let's go find the girl."

"Filth and maggots," Bernard cursed. "How do you know they haven't already caught her?"

"I just . . . know." All of Ross's senses seemed stronger tonight. Somewhere in the distance, he heard the pawing of a horse's hooves. He could almost feel Lord Damon peering into the blackness, trying to find the girl. Ross could smell the sweat and thrill of the hunt as the wolves slinked through the darkness.

"We've got to find her before they do," Ross told his friend.

Bernard just shook his head. "Sometimes, Ross, I think you're right out of your head."

The two friends had been searching for nearly an hour when Ross heard the snap of a twig. He froze and peered into the darkness.

That's when he saw the girl again. She was crouched behind a thorn bush. The moonlight was reflected in her eyes as she saw him approach. Ross sensed that she wanted to run, but a wolf was sniffing the ground not ten feet from where she hid.

The girl turned her head to where the wolf crouched low. Then she turned to stare at Ross with wild eyes. They seemed to plead with him. *Help me!*

Ross motioned silently to Bernard.

Like a great clumsy beast, Bernard thundered into the clearing. He waved his burning torch wildly at the wolf. Then he shouted, "Run off, you devil, run!"

The wolf yelped and backed away. Then it bolted off into the woods.

Ross was beside the girl in a flash. He took her by the arm. "Don't worry. We're here to help you. We won't let you fall into Lord Damon's hands."

"Thank you," the girl whispered. Then she looked into Ross's eyes and smiled.

"All right, you two," Bernard barked. "Let's get a move on. You can get all starry-eyed once we get out of here."

It was Bernard who led the others back to town. He was clumsy, and sometimes got lost, but somehow found a way through the woods. Just outside of town, he gestured for the girl to stay back. Bernard wanted a few words with Ross — and Ross alone.

"So what's your plan?" Bernard asked.

"Plan?"

"You saved the girl, didn't you?" Bernard asked. "So

what's next? You can't just put her on a cart and send her off to the next town."

"Maybe Uncle Axel . . ." Ross began.

"Forget it," Bernard snapped back. He had to force back a laugh.

"Well, somehow she has to get back to her people," Ross told him.

Bernard turned to look at his friend. "And who are her people? You know nothing about this girl, my friend. Maybe she really is a thief. Maybe she's a witch."

"She was in trouble," Ross replied.

"And maybe the girl *is* trouble," Bernard told him. "Something about her seems strange to me." He stopped and looked back at the girl. "I don't trust her. And I don't think you should trust her, either."

CHAPTER THREE | I Am Not a Thief!

Ross couldn't come up with a plan. But he knew the girl had to spend the night someplace. The best place, or so it seemed, was in Uncle Axel's stable. Perhaps the next day, when the sun shone, Ross would come up with something better. Perhaps the strange girl would explain herself. But, for now, they all needed to get some sleep.

Bernard stopped when the group reached the stable door. Bernard looked back at the girl and whispered to his friend, "She sure is easy on the eyes, ain't she." He didn't wait for Ross to reply. "But remember what I said before. You be careful." Then he gave Ross a quick wink and was gone.

When Ross took the girl into the stables, the horses made nervous noises. They side-stepped in their stalls and shook their manes.

"Don't let them bother you," Ross said. "Strangers sometimes scare them." He patted the horses' necks and calmed them.

"So this is it?" the girl asked. "You think I'll be safe here?"

"Unless you have a better idea," Ross said. He pulled a rough blanket from a pile in the corner and laid it in an empty stall. "This is for you. I sleep in the corner over there." Ross pointed to a spot on the other side of the stable.

"You sleep in the stable?" She sniffed and crinkled her nose.

"My uncle owns the stable," Ross began. "But he and I don't get along."

"Why not?" the girl asked.

"It's a long story. I might tell it to you sometime. But first, you owe me your own story." Ross crossed his arms in front of his chest. "Why were Lord Damon and his wolves chasing you?"

"They think I'm a thief," she answered simply.

"And are you?"

She pressed her lips together. "No, I am not," she answered firmly. Then she yawned loudly. "I'm really tired and it's late. Can we talk more in the morning?"

Ross wanted to know more, but he could see dark circles under her eyes. The girl's skin looked even paler against the jet-black of her hair. She raised a hand to her mouth and yawned again.

"At least tell me your name," Ross said.

"It's Catherine. But all my friends call me Cat." The girl swayed a little as she spoke. Her run through the woods and the stress of the night were catching up with her.

"All right, Cat," Ross agreed, "get some sleep. But in the morning, I want to know everything. Then we'll figure out some way to get you home."

Cat curled up on the blanket that Ross had laid down for her. Within minutes, she was asleep. Then Ross snuffed the flame of his lantern. He lay down on his cot and prayed that this night he wouldn't dream.

But this night he would not even sleep.

~

Some hours after midnight, as he tossed on his cot, Ross heard the horses stir. The horses pawed the ground and pranced in their stalls. Ross knew they acted like this only when a fox or wolf was near. On this night, both might be true.

Ross got to his feet and lit his lantern. Then he thought of the girl.

"Cat, are you . . . ?" Ross didn't get to finish his sentence. In the stall where Cat had fallen asleep, there was only a blanket.

Ross ran to the stable door and looked outside. A huge black shadow moved just outside of his lantern's light.

Ross froze. The shadow was much bigger than a wolf's. Was it a bear? Ross froze. He remembered what Bernard's Pa had said about a great black beast. Carefully, he reached for the pitchfork just inside the door.

But what came out of the forest was neither a wolf nor a bear. It was Cat. She walked back to the stable and smiled sweetly at Ross. "I hope I didn't worry you."

"Where were you?" Ross peered over her shoulder. The dark shadow was now gone. It must have run off at the sound of their voices.

"Nature called," Cat said. "I didn't want to wake you."

She's lying, said a voice inside Ross's head. But Ross looked into the girl's smiling eyes and ignored the warning. "Well, you'd better be more careful next time," Ross warned her. "I saw something at the edge of the woods. It had the horses scared."

Once again, Cat just gave him a smile.

~

In the morning, Ross had work to do. He took two pails from the stable and went down to the well. After filling them, he went back to make feed for the horses.

Just as Ross stepped back through the stable doors, he saw something moving inside. Putting down the water pails, he crept to the small nook where he had been trying to sleep.

There, in front of him, was Cat.

"Looking for something?" Ross asked.

He'd caught her, that much was sure. The girl must have been going through his pack. Half his clothes lay strewn on the floor.

Cat looked up at Ross with wide eyes. "Oh dear. How this must look!" She smiled sweetly. "I was only looking for a comb. You weren't here, and so I thought . . . ." She showed him the tangles in her long black hair.

"A comb," Ross said. "Looking for a comb." Even as he repeated the words, Ross couldn't believe them.

Ross ran his fingers through his wild red hair. "Do I look like I own a comb?" Ross was about to lecture her about stealing. Then he saw a silk bundle in her hand.

My mother's ring, Ross thought. He felt his blood start to boil.

Quickly Ross ripped the silk bundle from her hand. He unfolded the small square of fabric and gave a loud sigh of relief. His mother's ring was still there.

"Is this how you repay me for helping you?" Ross

asked. "By stealing from me?"

Cat leapt to her feet in one graceful move. She made a strange sound, like air being forced through her teeth. It was almost a hiss. Her eyes were wild and challenging. "I am not a thief!"

"That's not how it looks from here," Ross squared off against her. He was beyond anger now. How dare she go through his things! How dare she touch the ring itself!

"I can explain . . . ." Cat began, but she had no chance to finish. Outside the stable, Ross could hear his uncle calling.

"Useless boy!" his uncle shouted. "Get your lazy behind out here. We have a visitor. A gentleman. And he needs some help."

Ross was torn. What to do? If Uncle Axel found Cat in here, he'd turn her over to Lord Damon's men. He might turn in Ross himself. But what was this girl doing going through his things? Maybe he should have listened to Bernard last night. Maybe Cat was a thief.

But there was no time to think on all that.

"Hide!" Ross whispered

He pushed Cat to the floor and covered her with his clothes and blankets. He could only hope that his uncle wouldn't come looking inside the stable.

CHAPTER FOUR | Hide!

When Ross got outside, he could not believe what he saw. In front of him stood the most beautiful horse he had ever seen. Its hide was white as buttermilk. But its mane and tail were fiery red.

Uncle Axel stood beside the horse with a wide smile on his face. A big bag of coins was jingling in his meaty palm.

"Take care of this good man's horse, boy," Uncle Axel said. "His horse only gets the best. Do you hear, boy?" He jingled the bag of coins again under Ross's nose.

"Uncle . . . " Ross stuttered, "this is a Fire Mare."

"Of course it's a Fire Mare," his uncle said. "Don't you think that I know good horse flesh when I see it, boy?" Uncle Axel's friendly tone didn't match the force he used to grab Ross's arm. Ross winced from the pain but kept from crying out.

"Of course, Uncle," Ross answered. The pain ebbed as Uncle released his arm.

The stranger smiled and tossed Ross a coin from his pouch. "Her name is Nina," the stranger said. "Take good care of her while I'm working in town."

"Yes, sir," Ross promised as he caught the coin. He knew it wouldn't be his for long. Uncle Axel would see to that.

Ross patted the mare's neck to coax her inside. A small jolt, like lightning, moved through his hand and up his arm. For a moment, his vision blurred and his head spun. Ross blinked his eyes and the feeling was gone. He shook his head. Then he led the mare into a clean stall.

Uncle Axel came in at the same moment. Ross panicked, afraid that his uncle might find Cat if he looked around the stable. But Uncle Axel didn't care about that.

"The coin, boy," he said, putting out his hand.

"Oh, yes, of course," Ross replied. Then he handed his uncle the stranger's coin.

"Take good care of this one," Uncle Axel warned him. "A Fire Mare can be dangerous. If she gets loose, this whole place could go up in flames."

"Yes, sir," Ross replied. But the Fire Mare was the least of his problems. The black-haired girl hiding in the stables was far worse.

~

It was past dinnertime before Ross was finally alone with Cat. "We need to be quiet. But I think it's safe for you to come out now."

Cat came out of the dark stall where she'd been hiding. She stretched her aching muscles in one long graceful move. Not for the first time, Ross thought that her nickname suited her.

Ross could no longer hold back the question that had been burning in his mind all day. "Who are you? And don't lie to me this time, Cat."

Cat lowered her eyes. "I told you the truth. My name *is* Catherine. My family lives on the other side of the forest. Lord Damon showed up at our door. He accused me of being a thief. So I ran." She rubbed the back of her neck. "You know they cut off a thief's hands, don't you?"

Ross imagined a guard's axe raised over Cat's arms. Then he shook the image from his mind. Ross wanted to believe Cat, but his inner voice kept warning Ross to be careful.

"And how did you manage to find my mother's ring?" Ross asked.

"I already told you that I was looking for a comb," Cat replied. "I didn't know the little bag held a ring. I was just holding it when you came back."

Ross looked at her and shook his head.

Cat smiled at him. "And why is the ring so important to you?" she asked. "Why do you keep it in a silk cloth? It must be very special."

Ross pulled the small piece of silk from his pocket. He cradled the bundle in his hand. "It was my mother's ring," he explained. "She died ten years ago, when I was six."

"That must have been terrible."

The memory came flooding into Ross's mind. "King Rudgerd's men raided our village one night. He heard that someone was hiding Skinwalkers, so he killed half our village as punishment."

"Skinwalkers?" Cat asked. "Your mother was killed for helping them?"

Ross felt the memory burn. He saw mother's frantic face as she placed the ring in his hand. "Hide it," she'd begged. "Keep it safe always." Then his mother kissed his frightened face. "Promise you won't let anyone take it from you. Someday you'll understand how important this is."

Ross had made his promise just before King Rudgerd's men broke down their door. As they dragged his mother away, he hid the ring in his mouth. "Remember!" his mother called as they tied her hands.

It was last time Ross saw his mother alive.

"Can I see the ring?" Cat asked.

"Why?" Ross snapped at her. "What's it to you?"

"I'm curious," Cat told him. "Just like a cat."

Ross didn't trust her, but saw no harm in taking the ring out of its silk case. He wouldn't let Cat touch the ring, but he could let her see it.

"It's beautiful," Cat said. "And there's writing on it."

"Old writing," Ross replied. "I've shown it to Bernard and a monk at the abbey, but no one knows how to read it."

"Maybe I can read it," Cat suggested.

Ross looked at her. "You?" What was the chance that a girl from another village could read this old writing?

"Just let me see it. My father reads most languages —

Human and Skinwalker. He believes that a girl should be able to read and write. I'm quite good at it, if I do say so myself."

Ross's inner voice said no, but somehow his hand reached out and offered the ring to Cat. Soon she was looking closely at the letters.

"It's Skinwalker writing," Cat told him. "From long ago."

Ross was surprised. Perhaps this girl knew more than she seemed to.

"And what does it say?"

Cat looked at him with wide eyes. "It says, 'Only the King shall possess this ring.'"

Ross shook his head and grabbed the ring back. "That's stupid," he told her. "You just made that up."

"It's the truth, Ross," Cat told him. "I have a hunch that ring is very, very special. You had better be careful with it."

Suddenly Ross was bone weary. He wanted nothing more than to fall into his cot and surrender to the forgetfulness of sleep. "That's enough talk for one night," he told Cat. "Get some sleep. Dawn comes early these days. Tomorrow we'll find some way to get you back home."

Ross removed his outer tunic and draped it on the

hook next to his cot. For a moment, his hand touched the small lump of his mother's ring. Ross felt a deep ache in his heart. "Keep it safe," his mother had pleaded. *I will*, thought Ross. *I promise*. He took the ring from his tunic, and held the silk in his hands. He was still holding the ring when he snuffed his lantern's light and all was dark.

Sleep came swiftly to Ross. But it wasn't a restful sleep. His mother's face called out to him, "Remember!" The sound of hooves running through the mist beat against his mind. Fire sprung from the ground. Wolves howled and snapped at his heels. The ring called his name — *Ross!*

Ross threw off his blanket and sprang to his feet. Sweat poured down his forehead and nose. His heart beat wildly. "Filth and maggots," he cursed as he sat back down on his cot. He cradled his aching head in his hands. "What's wrong with me?"

Ross's eyes began to adjust to the darkness. He looked over to where Cat should have been. All he saw was a crumpled blanket in the straw. "Cat!" he called as he ran to the stable door. "Are you there?"

Ross stumbled out into the night. The chill in the air made spirals of mist that snaked across the ground. The moon was high above. It cast an strange glow over the stable yard. Ross caught movement from the corner of his eye. He saw Cat's small form disappear into the wooded area behind the stable. What was she up to? Ross squared his shoulders and firmed his chin. Then he stepped quietly into the woods and after her.

In the glow of the moon's pale light, Ross was sure he saw her run into a small grove of ancient oaks. He rushed after her, tripping and cursing as roots and vines got in his way. How did she manage to run so gracefully in the dark?

Ross heard a twig snap as he reached the trunk of a giant old oak. "Aha!" he shouted as he stepped behind it. "I've got you . . . ."

The rest of his sentence froze in his throat. Ross's heart slowed, stopped and then sped up to an impossible pace. He swallowed hard and dared a look from side to side.

But there was no place to run.

A huge black panther bared its teeth and snarled. Its back arched. Its stomach was low to the ground. Its ears lay flat against its great black head. The panther was going to pounce.

I'm going to die, thought Ross.

CHAPTER FIVE | Beware

The panther bent low, ready to spring. Its eyes glared at Ross.

Ross crossed himself and began to pray. He braced himself for the attack. But the attack never came.

Suddenly, the panther soared over his head and landed on a branch. It leapt to the branch of the next oak and then the next. Within seconds, it was gone — lost in the night's shadow.

It took a moment for Ross's breathing to slow. His hands and knees shook. Ross knew he had to sit down. It was either that or fall down. He planted himself in the wet grass and waited for the shaking to stop. Ross didn't know how long he stayed there, pulling in great gulps of cool night air. An hour? Longer? When the chill and damp made his teeth chatter, Ross got shakily to his feet. He headed back to the warmth of the stable, thanking God that he was still alive but wondering if the panther were real.

And then he saw Catherine.

"There you are," Cat said sweetly. She stood in the middle of the stable. "I was getting worried. Where did you go?" She'd relit his lantern. Its light made her eyes glow a bright golden brown.

"Where did *I* go?" Ross was in no mood for Cat's lies. "You weren't here when I woke up. I went looking for *you!*"

Cat smiled an apology. "I couldn't sleep. I didn't want to wake you, so I went for a walk."

"Don't you know it's dangerous to go into the woods in the dark?" Ross shouted. He imagined Cat coming face to face with the hulking beast he'd just seen. "There's a panther prowling the woods. It could have killed you."

Cat's eyes grew so wide they almost swallowed her face. She lowered her head. "I didn't mean to worry you,

Ross. I'll remember to be more careful," she promised.

Rosse noticed again that Cat wouldn't meet his eyes. *Something isn't right here*, his inner voice said. Cat was hiding something. And Ross wasn't going to stop until he found out what it was.

Before he returned to bed, Ross calmed the horses in their stalls. They were always jumpy these days. With a panther in the woods, they had every reason to be.

Ross's heart pounded as he neared the Fire Mare's stall. Ross didn't like the way this horse made him feel. Sweat formed on his upper lip and forehead as he got close. His vision got blurry. His head pounded. Flashes of images ran before his eyes. Ross thought he heard the sound of hundreds of pounding hooves.

Ross pushed himself away from the Fire Mare's stall. It was past midnight now.

What was his uncle thinking, keeping a Fire Mare in the stable? They were dangerous. Their hooves had set many a farm on fire. Ross looked around him at the straw and worn boards of the stalls. It wouldn't take much to set this blazing. The stranger had paid Uncle well to board his horse. But was it worth the risk?

Ross turned to the stall where Cat lay sleeping. He gave a slow, tired smile. She looked so lost and helpless lying there. He had the urge to brush away a strand of hair that fell across her face. *She's beautiful,* he thought. *But trouble. Maybe those two always go together.*

Ross was still kneeling when his uncle burst through the stable doors. The old man stank of too much ale. He had a lantern in one hand and could easily see both Ross and Cat.

"What?" his uncle screamed. "What's this? A girl in here?"

He grabbed Ross by his neck and threw him to the floor.

"I thought they were joking at the tavern. They said a thief was hiding around here. The King's soldiers are looking all over for her. And here she is, in *my* stable."

He kicked at Cat's sleeping form. The kick sent her flying sideways.

"Get up, you little trollop. Get out of here before . . . "

But Uncle Axel didn't have time to finish. Outside there were voices and the sound of marching boots.

"Shhh," Uncle Axel whispered, but it was too late.

With a crash, the King's guards stormed into the stable.

Now Uncle Axel had a new plan. He smiled at the soldiers and said, "Here's your thief! My boy caught her for you. We've been holding her until you got here."

The soldiers just grunted in response. One of them

bent down and yanked Cat up by her hair. The girl screamed, but no one seemed to care except Ross.

Every part of Ross wanted to jump up and fight. But there were too many guards. They were armed and Ross had nothing to fight with. And there was only one way out of the stable — the small set of doors where more guards stood waiting. Ross wouldn't stand a chance.

So Ross watched helplessly as the guards led Cat away.

One guard stayed behind. "It's a shame, really. Such a fine-looking girl. Won't be nearly as pretty without her hands," he said. "But I think we can have some fun with her first." He winked and tossed Uncle Axel a handful of coins. "King Rudgerd rewards those who help bring them to justice."

Uncle Axel mumbled as he caught the coins, "Praise to the King." Then he followed the last guard out of the stable and into the night.

Ross slumped into a tired heap atop the straw. The guards were going to cut off Cat's hands! Sure, she'd get a trial first. But everyone knew what happened to people without enough money to buy their freedom. King Rudgerd's guards would make an example of Cat. And they didn't care if she was guilty or not.

I've got to help her, he thought. *But how?*

Ross couldn't leave the stable now. He could still hear the guards outside. His uncle must have passed around the keg of ale.

Ross got shakily to his feet. He felt like a thousand ants were crawling up his spine. His head spun. His stomach rolled. He leaned heavily against one of the stalls, trying to come up with a plan.

The Fire Mare's gleaming white face peered at him through the darkness. The horse nudged his cheek with its nose and snorted.

It sounded as if the horse said something. *Beware.*

Ross looked at the horse again, wondering if he was losing his mind.

Beware, came again.

All the air spilled from Ross's lungs. Outside, the King's guards were shouting. Inside, Ross heard the click of the stable door's latch. The door groaned softly open.

A shadowy figure came through the door. In the pale moonlight, Ross saw it was a hooded man. A hooded man with a very large knife.

CHAPTER SIX | Betrayed

In her stall, the Fire Mare snorted and stomped. She shook her wild red mane and whinnied. *Beware!*

"You!" the man in the cloak growled. He wasn't looking at Ross, but at the Fire Mare. "I should have known. Did you really think that you could save the girl?"

Ross stood frozen. He knew that voice. Long white hair flowed from beneath his hood. Moonlight caught the deathly white of his hands.

Lord Damon! What was he doing here?

Ross backed further into a stall. "You're too late. King

Rudgerd's guards have already taken her."

Lord Damon's laugh echoed through the stable. "Foolish boy. I didn't come for the girl. Why should I care about a girl?"

Lord Damon walked to the cot where Ross slept. He pulled Ross's tunic from the hook where Ross had hung it. Then he dug his pale white hand into the tunic's inner pocket.

"No!" Ross shouted.

Lord Damon pulled the small silk bundle and raised it high in his hands. "Right where Catherine told me it would be."

Ross felt like he'd been punched in the stomach.

"Ah, you didn't know she was working for me, did you?" Lord Damon said. Then he laughed and shook his fist at Ross. "Your family has had this ring much too long. It's mine now. And with you gone, there will be no one to stop me."

Lord Damon pulled the knife from under his cloak and raised it high. The long blade shone silver in the moonlight.

Ross put up his hands, as if his hands alone could stop the knife.

But Ross never had to use his hands. At that moment, the Fire Mare snorted in her stall. She pulled back her upper lip and bared her teeth. The ground shook as she bucked and stomped. She struck her hooves hard against the ground.

Lord Damon stopped, his eyes drawn by the noise.

Suddenly, flames burst out from beneath the Fire Mare. Straw ignited. Wood smoked and then crackled into flame.

Fire! The stable was on fire!

Lord Damon backed away and placed the ring in his mouth. He dropped the knife and looked at the flames with terror.

At that moment, Lord Damon's eyes grew wide. He growled and bared sharp white teeth. And then his face began to shift and change. Lord Damon's jaw stretched and grew. Large pointed ears sprouted from his head. His body shifted and shook. His human skin was replaced with coarse white hair.

Within seconds, Lord Damon had become a snarling white wolf. Lord Damon, the King's trusted advisor, was a Skinwalker!

The wolf backed away from the fire, its eyes frantic. "You fiery witch," it snarled. "Don't make the mistake of thinking you've won. This is only the beginning." Then the wolf bounded through the stable doors and was lost in the darkness.

Ross stood frozen as the fire in the stable spread from stall to stall. Two things buzzed around in his brain. *Lord Damon was a Skinwalker. Cat had betrayed him.*

The sound of frantic horses brought him to his senses. Ross had to move. He had to try to save the horses. Soon he was running through the stable, opening stalls and untying horses. When all the horses were freed, Ross pushed his way through the smoke and flames. He hurried out into the first blush of morning's light.

The yard outside was filled with drunken guards and running villagers. They shouted and stared at him and the fire. Ross imagined how he must have looked to them, framed in the fire's light.

"You useless . . . ." his uncle swore.

"It's that devil boy," one villager shouted. "He must have done this himself. He must have set the fire."

There was a loud whinny and Ross looked to one side. There was the Fire Mare, waiting for him. *Get up,* she seemed to say. *Get away.*

Somehow Ross lifted himself onto the mare's back. She reared up, fighting off Uncle Axel with her hooves. Then she was in the clear and heading towards the forest.

Dazed, Ross dared one look back. The stables were engulfed in flames. There, watching from a crest on the hill stood a great white wolf.

Beneath him, the Fire Mare's muscles pumped as she ran. Flames licked at her hooves.

Where was she taking him? And what would happen to him next?

CHAPTER SEVEN | A Rescue

Ross and the Fire Mare followed the marshlands to skirt around the forest. The marsh's tall grasses hid them behind a curtain of green. "Where are you taking me?" Ross asked.

The mare shook her mane and snorted. She'd circled the bottom tip of the forest and was heading east. Soon Ross caught the smell of seawater. His shoulders tensed when an outcrop of rocks came into view. "Why are you taking me back to the village?"

The mare sidestepped and shook her mane. Then she

knelt and leaned forward until Ross had no choice but to dismount. "Why are we stopping here?" Ross cried. "What is this all about?"

Ross's words were cut off by a large hand clamped firmly over his mouth.

"Unnnh," Ross grunted, his words muffled.

Then Ross heard a voice he knew well. "If you don't keep your voice down, Carrot Head, the whole village will know you're back."

Bernard released Ross as quickly as he'd grabbed him. The two friends stared at each other, both amazed.

"What are you doing back here?" Bernard asked. "Don't you know that your uncle has all the King's guards looking for you? They blame you for the fire at the stable."

"Why am I back?" Ross replied. "Ask her." He pointed toward the Fire Mare.

Bernard's eyes grew wide. He looked at Ross as if his friend had just grown another head.

"You want me to ask a horse? Don't you think that's a little . . . strange?"

"You won't think anything's strange after I tell you about last night."

"Inside here," Bernard told him, pushing him into a shed, "where we can't be seen. And this story had better

be a good one, not just one of your strange dreams."

It took Ross the better part of an hour to explain it all. The guards finding Cat. Lord Damon taking the ring. Cat working for Lord Damon. The warning from the Fire Mare and the fire itself. It was all too much for Bernard to take in.

"Lord Damon . . . a Skinwalker. I can't believe it," said Bernard once Ross had finished. "Pa said them Skinwalkers wouldn't stay in hiding forever. Next thing you know, they'll be sending an army to take over the towns. Wouldn't that be something?"

Ross could only shake his head. If the Skinwalkers took over, how much bloodshed would there be? King Rudgerd was cruel, but the Skinwalkers weren't even human.

Bernard put his arm around Ross's shoulder. "And who'd have thought that girl was working for Lord Damon? I told you she was trouble, didn't I? You should listen to your old buddy when I tell you something." Then he slapped Ross hard on the back. "So, what's the plan?"

"Plan?"

"How are we going to get your mother's ring back? And how do we stop the guards from cutting off Cat's pretty hands?" Bernard stood with his arms folded in front of him.

"*We* aren't going to do anything," Ross answered hotly. "I'm in enough trouble already without dragging you into this. None of this is your fight, Bernard."

"That's a terrible thing to say to a friend." Bernard dug in his heels. "You'd be a fool to chase after Lord Damon alone. You may be fast, Ross, but I'm stronger and better in a fight." He raised a hand to silence Ross before he could argue. "Face it — you need me."

The mare snorted and nodded her head. So the choice was made.

Bernard hurried home to collect supplies and a pack

for each of them. He was back in no time, panting from the weight of two packs on his back.

"What did you tell your Pa?" Ross asked.

"Not to worry. The old man is understanding in these things. We'd best be on our way. No need to waste the morning light."

~

As they rode south on the Fire Mare, Ross did come up with a plan. The real goal was to get Ross's ring back from Lord Damon. But the two of them had no way of finding the Dark Lord unless they had help. And the only person who might know where Lord Damon would be was in the stockade. And she was waiting for her hands to be cut off.

The mare retraced the trail of ash she'd left behind from the night before. When they reached the stockade, Ross and Bernard left her grazing just inside the woods. They traveled the rest of the distance on foot.

Then they had a stroke of good luck. It was lunch time, and most of the guards were off eating. Only a single guard was watching the stockade door. Even from this distance, Ross could hear the rustle of mail, the clink of armor every time the guard moved.

"There," Bernard whispered. "Now we just have to

get past him. Any ideas?"

Ross looked around quickly. He felt so alive since the wild ride on the mare. His senses were heightened. "Follow my lead," Ross told him. "And remember your Pa's wrestling lessons," Ross whispered. Then the two of them slipped around the north of the stockade.

Ross waited until he heard the guard step forward. Then Ross raced in front to distract him. At the same time, Bernard approached from behind. The trap was set.

Bernard wrapped his arms around the guard's throat and squeezed. His Pa had shown him how to cut off a man's air like this. If he timed it right, there was no real harm done. In ten seconds, the guard was out cold. They dragged him behind a nearby bush and tied his hands and feet. Then Ross took the guard's sword and tucked it into his belt. Bernard took his knife.

"So far, so good," said Bernard. "What's now?"

"Why do I have to do all the thinking?"

"Because you're the brains and I'm the brawn," Bernard said. "The brains think and the brawn does the work. Simple as that."

"So now we break in and rescue Cat," Ross replied simply. "Then use her to find Lord Damon."

"Sounds easy," Bernard said. "Let's go."

Ross and Bernard entered the stockade. They found Cat in a corner with her hands and feet tied.

Cat looked up as she saw them enter. "Ross, you fool! What are doing here?"

"I've come for my ring," Ross muttered. "I have a hunch you know exactly where it is." He began to untie her.

"Don't you fret," Bernard reassured her. "I'm with him. Ain't nothing to worry about right now. When the morning comes, you'll still have two pretty hands."

Cat's face froze. "No!" she hissed. She looked from Ross to Bernard. Then she shook her head and pointed to the door.

One of the King's guards stood in the doorway. "In here!" he shouted.

The guard raced in and drew his sword. In seconds, he was followed by four more guards.

Ross gripped his stolen sword. Bernard stood beside him, shifting his knife from hand to hand.

"So . . . what's the new plan?" Bernard asked.

CHAPTER EIGHT
The Great Black Beast

"The new plan is simple — count on the brawn," Ross answered.

Bernard grunted, "Well, that makes me feel better." Then he charged the guards like an angry bear.

Ross thrust his sword, gave a loud shout and rushed forward beside his friend.

Blades clanked as they fought the five men. Ross's muscles felt the weight of each blow from his sword. He swung his blade wildly with both hands. It took every bit of his skill just to counter the attack from two of the guards. His breath became ragged as he blocked and thrust. How long could he keep going?

From the corner of his eye, Ross could see Bernard barrel through a trio of guards like a raging bull. Bernard shouted and cursed as he swung his knife. Slowly the guards backed away.

But Ross should not have been watching. That split second glancing at Bernard was all the time his two guards needed. The tip of one guard's blade grazed Ross's chest. The butt of the second guard's sword slammed Ross in the stomach. The blow sent him flying. Ross crashed against the rear wall of the stockade. *Thud*. His ears rang. His head spun. The thin cut in his chest sent blood onto his tunic.

"Ross, no!" Bernard shouted.

As soon as Bernard looked away, he was done for. One guard broke a stool across the back of Bernard's head. Bernard fell facedown in a heap on the floor. Then a second guard loomed above Bernard. His sword was raised to deliver a killing blow.

"This will teach a fisherman's son his place." The guard smiled and placed his boot on the small of Bernard's back.

Ross closed his eyes. He couldn't watch his friend's death. But the sound of an angry roar came first.

There was a panther in the stockade!

The huge black panther jumped on the guard who stood over Bernard. It sunk its teeth into the man's throat and then shook him until his body went limp. Then the panther turned and leapt at the remaining guards.

The stockade echoed with their screams. Two of the guards managed to escape, but two others cringed in a corner waiting for death. They did not have long to wait.

Ross crawled to where Bernard lay. He turned him onto his back and shook him. "Please, Bernard," he begged. "You've got to get up before that beast gets us. We've got to get out of here."

Bernard only moaned in pain.

Ross wrapped Bernard's arm around his neck. He placed his shoulder under Bernard's armpit and pushed up. He tried shakily to pull Bernard to his feet, but it was like trying to lift a mountain. Every muscle in Ross's body ached from the effort. He looked to the only door out of the stockade.

Then Ross froze.

The panther stood in the light of the doorway. It turned its head slowly as it looked around the room. Then it stared straight into Ross's eyes.

"Hurry, you fool! There'll be more guards soon

enough," said a female voice. "We need to get away."

Ross let Bernard's slack body fall to the floor.

"Catherine?"

The panther tread to where Ross stood. It bumped him with its nose. "We have to leave now!"

Ross backed away in fear.

"Fine. You stay here, then. I can save your friend, but not both of you." Then the panther took Bernard's tunic in its mouth. She started dragging him to the door.

Ross cradled his aching head. It all made a crazy kind of sense. Why the horses in the stable were always so nervous when Cat was around. Why she disappeared each night. Why the panther in the woods hadn't attacked him.

The panther *was* Cat.

Cat was a Skinwalker!

"Are you coming?" asked Cat as she dragged Bernard out the door.

~

The strange group stopped when they reached the stream. The Fire Mare was grazing nearby.

"We should rest here for a while and see to your wounds," said Cat.

Ross couldn't get used to the female voice coming from this great black panther. Ross searched for words. "I . . . don't understand."

"What part don't you understand? That I'm really a Skinwalker, or that I just saved your life?" Cat paced between the trees as she talked. "Of all people, I thought at least *you* would understand."

"Why me?" Ross spread his arms wide. "I'm just a stable boy."

"No," answered Cat. "You are much more than that."

Suddenly they heard another female voice, shrill and angry. "No, Cat. Don't."

"He has a right to know," Cat argued.

"He's not ready yet and you know it," answered the other voice.

"Who's there?" Ross raised his sword even though blood still oozed from his chest. "Show yourself."

"She can't." Cat laughed loudly. It sounded somewhere between a belly laugh and a growl.

Ross's head was aching badly. "She can't what?"

"She can't show herself."

"Why not?" Ross kept looking into the trees to see if he could spot her.

"Because she's naked." Cat laughed again. "Come to think of it, so am I. Do you have an extra tunic I could borrow? It would be easier to tend your wounds if I could use my hands."

Ross felt his stomach turn flips. He had to sit down. "In the pack, over there." He pointed to where they'd hidden their packs earlier.

"Thank you." Ross watched as Cat's paw stretched and shrunk. Then small human fingers wiggled at the end of her furry black leg. She picked the pack up with her newly formed hand and padded to a thick crop of bushes.

Moments later, Cat emerged — not as a panther — but as herself. She had a blanket wrapped around her pale body and tied at the back of her neck. "Not exactly the latest fashion." She grinned as she ran her fingers through her tangled hair. "But at least I'm covered."

Then Cat bent down and examined the wound on the back of Bernard's head. "This doesn't look too bad. I saw some herbs on the way here that will heal this. He just needs to rest." She gently placed the pack under Bernard's head. Then she headed toward Ross. "Now let me see that cut in your chest."

Ross backed away. This was still all too strange for him.

"Don't be a fool, Ross," Cat told him. "That needs to be cleaned or it will start to fester."

Ross was too tired and sore to argue. He let her clean and bandage his wounds. When she had finished, he heard the sound of a woman clearing her voice.

"And what about me?" the other female voice asked.

Cat glanced back over her shoulder. "What about you?"

"I could use some help here." The voice was annoyed.

Cat laughed and pulled a tunic from Bernard's pack. She draped it over the Fire's Mare's back. "Hurry up, then. We need to get moving as soon as Bernard is awake."

The Fire Mare walked off into the crop of bushes.

Ross was beginning to understand. Still, his logical mind couldn't believe it. That is, not until he saw the Fire Mare returned.

The girl looked ridiculous in Bernard's oversized tunic. Ridiculous and lovely. The Fire Mare had turned into one of the most beautiful girls Ross had ever seen. Her skin was as very pale and her wild red hair flowed down her back.

She scrunched her nose and pouted. "Are you sure this tunic is the best you could do?" she asked Cat.

"Unless you've got a clothing stash nearby, it will have to do." Cat laughed, enjoying the other woman's discomfort. Then she sobered up. "Don't worry, there's a clothing stash on the way to the camp. We can change our clothes then."

Ross felt like his head was going to explode. "STOP!" he shouted. "Who *are* you people? What clothing stash? And, on the way to where?"

"The answer to your first question, I think you've already figured out," said the redheaded woman. "We're Skinwalkers. I saved you from Lord Damon and carried you here." She waited for the information to sink in. "Cat saved you from the guards."

Then Cat spoke. "We keep stashes of clothes hidden in various places." Ross looked at her with a blank expression. "Animals don't wear clothes. People do. So when we're in human form, we need clothes."

"I guess," Ross replied, still amazed.

"It's not smart for a Skinwalker to carry around clothes when walking in their animal skin. Too many One-Skins are only too happy to kill a Skinwalker."

"One-Skins?" Ross felt like he'd fallen into one of his crazy dreams.

"Humans. Like your friend Bernard." The redhead pointed to where Bernard lay. "Humans have only one skin. Skinwalkers have two."

Ross could hardly believe all this. Was this really happening? Could animals transform into humans and back again? How? How was any of this possible?

The girl ignored his confusion. "Which brings up the next problem. What are we going to do with him?"

"He's coming with us." Cat folded her arms.

"But he's a One-Skin!"

A growl came from deep in Cat's throat. She took a threatening step forward. "Bernard risked his life to save me. We are not leaving him behind."

The redheaded girl backed away. "He won't be very welcome."

"Let me deal with that." Cat turned to Ross who stood with his jaw hanging open. "As for your third question." She placed a hand on his shoulder. "We're taking you to the Skinwalkers' camp. Because that's where *you* belong."

CHAPTER NINE | The Ring

Ross brushed Cat's hand from his shoulder. He was still angry with Cat. "You have to be joking," Ross faced off against her. "I'm not going anywhere with you or anyone else until I get some answers."

"I can understand why you might be upset . . . " Cat began.

"Upset? You helped Lord Damon steal my mother's ring. Why, Cat? What's so important about my mother's ring? Why did Lord Damon want it? Why did you help him? And this time, no more lies!" Ross felt his anger

flow up his neck and into his red face.

The redhead answered well before Cat could. "Why? Because Catherine placed her own needs over the good of her people."

"It's not like that at all and you know it, Nina," Cat snapped back. Cat turned to Ross with wide, pleading eyes. "Lord Damon has my brother locked in his dungeon. He said he'd kill him if I didn't get the ring."

Nina shook her head. "You seem to forget that the ring is important to us all. Now that Lord Damon has it, so you've tipped the scale in his favor." Nina placed her hands on her hips. "A war is coming, you selfish little cat. And you may have given Lord Damon his one chance to win it."

Cat moved with a speed that startled Ross. She pushed Nina up against a tree. Her panther roar startled the nearby birds into frantic flight. "Little cat, eh? Let's see if you think so once I'm done with you."

"STOP THIS!" Ross shouted. "No good will come from you two arguing. And you still haven't explained why Lord Damon wants the ring."

"You really don't know?" Cat released Nina. She turned to Ross and looked at him. "Ross, what do you remember about your mother and the ring?"

Ross felt an ache deep in the pit of his stomach. He tried to picture his mother's face. "I remember she gave me the ring just before the guards took her away. She said it was important that I hide it. She said someday I'd understand."

"Ross, your mother left behind her home and her people for your safety." She paused so her next words would sink in. "I guess she never told you. But your mother didn't belong among the One-Skins . . . any more than you do."

"What are you talking about?" Ross kept pacing as he

spoke. "My mother was human. So am I."

Cat looked deep into Ross's eyes. "No, Ross, you're not."

Nina pushed herself away from the tree. Now it was her turn to explain. "Your mother was the daughter of our King. During a terrible raid, King Rudgerd's guards killed many of the males of our clan. It was only a few days later that your mother gave birth to you. She was afraid that the same thing would happen to you."

Ross bowed his head. He walked to a fallen tree where he could sit down. His legs shook badly.

"Your mother left our clan to live among the One-Skins to keep you safe," Nina continued. "She passed herself off as one of them. She pretended that *you* were one of them." Nina took his trembling hand in hers. "Surely you must have guessed that you were different."

Ross thought about his dreams. He thought about his sense that something was missing in his life. Some part of him had always known he didn't belong. "But that would make me . . . ."

"A Skinwalker," Nina finished for him. "Like me, one of the Fire Steed Clan. One of the few remaining male Fire Steeds."

Ross felt as if all the air had been whooshed out of his lungs. Could it be true? "Let's say that I believe you." He swallowed hard to keep his voice from shaking. "What does this have to do with the ring? Why does Lord Damon want it?"

Nina went on. "The ring is a symbol of power for all the clans of Skinwalkers. Whoever wears it rules us."

"So, Lord Damon wants to rule all the Skinwalkers?"

"Yes," Cat told him. "He wants the power and he wants a war."

"A war?"

"Against One-Skins. A war to enslave all the humans. Lord Damon hates One-Skins. He wants to use the ring to force all the Skinwalkers to join him. Then he'll put together an army to wage war against the humans."

"Can he do that?" Ross asked.

"Yes, he can," Cat explained. "The ring can be only worn by someone in the family of a Skinwalker King. With the slaughter of our clans, there are only two of those people left. Lord Damon is one of them."

"You said that my mother was the daughter of your King." Ross's heart beat wildly.

"That makes *you* the other one, Ross," Cat replied. "Or perhaps I should say Your Highness."

CHAPTER TEN | Skinwalkers

Ross tried to make sense of all he'd learned. He was a Skinwalker! The thought of it scared and excited him all at the same time. What was it like to run on four legs? To speed like lightning across a field?

Ross's head reeled with questions. He looked into Nina's worried face. She'd said that a war was brewing. Ross put his curiosity aside. Instead, he asked, "Now that Lord Damon has the ring, what will he do?"

"My guess is that he's already gathering an army to march against the One-Skins." Nina shook her head sadly. "Of course, the Wolf Clan is faithful to his cause. He is their leader. But there are many more clans that he'll recruit now that he has the ring."

"Then we have to get it back."

"I hoped you'd feel that way." Nina smiled and nodded. "But we can't do it alone. And you're not ready yet. You must also be trained in our Skinwalker ways. Our King must be a Skinwalker himself."

"Yes, I understand," Ross told her.

"Will you come join us at our camp?"

When Ross nodded, Nina gave him a quick hug. "I'll travel ahead then. To let them know you're coming."

Ross watched Nina disappear behind a bush. When she came out, she was a horse once again. She shook her wild red mane and pranced. "Keep him safe," she called to Cat.

A low growl came from deep in Cat's throat. "Run quick, Nina. Leave Ross's safety to me."

"We'll meet again soon," Nina promised Ross. Then she raced off into the west.

At that moment, there was a groan and a laugh off to one side. "Well, if that don't beat all!" Bernard said. He still lay with his head on one of the packs.

Ross rushed to his side. "How do you feel?"

"Like a pretty mean horse kicked me in the head,"

Bernard answered as he sat up.

"How much of our talk did you hear?"

"Enough to know that there's a fight coming." Bernard got shakily to his feet. "And you're going to need all the help you can get."

Ross offered his friend his shoulder to steady him. "This is much more dangerous than anything we've done so far . . . ."

"Don't you go telling me that it's not my fight." Bernard refused Ross's offer of help to stand up. "It seems to me that my One-Skin people have as much at stake here as yours."

"Mine?"

"Your Skinwalker people," Bernard replied. "I always thought you were weird, my friend, but now it makes some sense."

Cat laughed at that. She had watched it all from the shade of a nearby oak. "I guess that means it's time to pack up." She shoved their few belongings into the two packs and tossed one to Bernard. The second, she slung on her back. As she headed off towards the west, she stopped to look over her shoulder. "What are you two waiting for? Let's go."

Then the three of them headed off to find the Skinwalker's camp.

They tramped through the woods in silence. Ross still had a thousand questions running through his head, but Cat was in no mood to answer. She paced moodily in front. A low growl came from her as they came to a twisted oak along the trail. She dug beneath the dead leaves around its roots. Within minutes she had a worn pack in her hands.

"A clothing stash! At last, real clothes!" she called over her shoulder. "Wait here a moment." Then Cat disappeared behind a bush. When she came out, she wore a simple brown dress with a wide red sash tied around the hips.

"Wow!" Bernard whistled. "You look great. What's the occasion?"

"If I'm going to march to my own funeral, I may as well look good." Cat slung the pack over her shoulder.

"What do you mean?" Ross asked.

"You heard Nina. I helped Lord Damon get your ring. Nina isn't the only one who's going to blame me for that."

"Then why are you helping us?"

"Because it's the right thing to do." She turned to Ross and folded her arms like battle swords in front of her chest. "And maybe I like you, stupid as you are."

Ross suddenly felt his cheeks turn red.

"But I'll only take you as far as the Skinwalker camp. I still have to save my brother."

"Cat, I can understand why you did what you did. Bernard is the closest I've got to a brother. If Lord Damon had him trapped, I probably would do the same." Then Ross took her trembling hand into his. "Why can't we work together? You can take us to the Skinwalker's camp. Then stay and help us figure out how to get the ring from Lord Damon. In return, we'll help you get your brother back. I give you my word."

"Don't mistake me for some helpless girl," she warned him. "I can do a lot worse than scratch your eyes out."

"I saw what you did to those guards. But face it, Cat, we stand a better chance together than we do alone."

"All right then. We stand together."

~

They reached the Skinwalker camp just before dusk. Cat fell silent the last few miles of their trek. Ross saw the tension in her shoulders as she marched them to a group of sentries who blocked their path. But Cat wasn't alone in being afraid. The hairs at the back of Ross's neck rose. He'd never seen anything like this.

A brown bear stood beside a tall, doe-like woman

with an archer's bow over her shoulder. A fat man with tusks glared at them. Foxes and elk stood with men in brown tunics.

"Seb is expecting us," Cat growled. She took a step forward in a threatening way. Ross watched the sentries back away nervously.

"Seb is expecting *him*," the man with tusks corrected. He pointed at Ross. "Not the other one. You have nerve bringing a One-Skin into our camp, She-cat." Anger and distrust flowed like a wave from him.

"Bernard is my friend," Ross stepped in front of Bernard. "Where I go, he goes."

"Bravely put, if not wisely," answered an old voice.

The sentries parted to allow their leader to step through. Ross tried not to stare. But how could he not? The man who came forward had the huge antlers of a stag growing from his head, but still he was a man.

"My name is Seb. And I've waited a long time to meet you, young friend." He placed a hand on Ross's shoulder.

Ross's eyes grew wide as full moons as Seb bowed low.

"Ah, these." Seb smiled and touched his antlers. "Sometimes I forget that they're there." Ross watched open-mouthed as the antlers quickly disappeared.

"You!" Ross suddenly recognized him. "You're the

stranger who brought the Fire Mare, I mean Nina, to the stables."

"Correct. We feared that Lord Damon would try to kill you once he had the ring. Nina was our best chance to get close without the One-Skins knowing."

"She probably saved my life."

"And Cat, as well," Seb agreed. "It has always been my wish that you and I should be friends, Ross. I have been waiting for the moment when you find your true self. So it is with regret that I do what I must."

Seb snapped his fingers. A dozen arrows were pointed at Ross, Bernard and Cat. "Take the One-Skin into a cave and bind him. Place a guard outside." He turned and his voice boomed. "No one is to harm him. Is that understood?"

The sentries nodded their heads in agreement. Three of them marched Bernard away. The remaining sentries pointed their arrows at Ross and Cat.

CHAPTER ELEVEN | Changing Skins

"No! You can't do this," Ross pleaded with the Skinwalker leader. "If it wasn't for my friend Bernard, I never would have made it this far. He is a true and good friend."

"Your friend is a One-Skin. That is enough for most of our camp to distrust him. You must believe me, Ross. I do this as much for his protection as theirs." He leaned to whisper in Ross's ear. "I may lead our group, but I can't always control them. I am not a King, unlike you. But no harm will come to Bernard if he's kept out of sight."

Ross shook his head but saw the wisdom in Seb's words. What else could he do? "And what about Cat?"

"Ah yes, Catherine." Seb closed his eyes as though he were suddenly very tired. "I do not agree with her recent actions. But her heart is true. And she did bring you to us."

The old man turned to Cat. "Lord Damon believes you to be loyal to him. We may be able to use that to help our cause. Still, I have a question for you, young Catherine. Where *do* your loyalties lie?"

"They have always been with my people," Cat's voice faltered. Then she gave a loud roar. "Ross promised to help me rescue my brother when we go after the ring. I pledge my loyalty and my life to that end."

Seb raised his right hand. He spoke loudly so that all would hear. "We are too few not to accept the help of a skillful warrior such as Catherine. Perhaps there will come a chance for her to right her wrong."

Then Seb placed his arm around Ross's shoulder. "Come, it grows late. You must eat and rest. Tomorrow we begin your training. Only a true Skinwalker can be King of our people."

~

For days, Ross trained with many teachers to learn the ways of a Skinwalker. Each night he would creep into the cave where Bernard was held. He brought food, water and as much comfort as he could.

Bernard accepted the turn of events with his usual good nature. "I can understand why some of them might not trust me. King Rudgerd's painted most humans with a black brush, if you ask me. But Pa's always been good to their kind." He leaned in close to whisper, "Pa's hid a few Skinwalkers in his time from Rudgerd's butchers.

When I asked him about the danger, he says, *sometimes a man's just got to do what a man's got to do.*" He winked and nodded. "Don't you worry about me."

So Ross put all his effort into his training. By the end of the second day, Ross experienced his first full change. His skin tingled as if a sword were sliding up and down his back. His vision blurred, then changed. There was a feeling, like stepping sideways through the air. Ross's jaw stretched. His eyes widened and shifted farther apart. Fingers and toes joined and hardened until they became hooves. His legs and arms stretched and bent.

It was exciting. And it was terrifying.

Ross shook his red mane. He looked back to see his white muscled body and long red tail. "I did it!" he shouted. Ross broke into a full gallop. Within three steps, he stumbled and fell into a muddy pool.

"Not so fast." Nina tried to cover her laugh. Ross was sprawled, up to his rump, in the mud. "You've never run on four legs before. It will take time before you get used to it." She helped Ross up. "Everything you experience will feel different now that you've changed skins. Your vision. Your sense of smell. Some changes will come naturally. Others, you will need training in order to use them. Most important, you must learn to control the fire when you run. While fire has its uses, it's also dangerous."

By the fourth day, Ross could run as well as any member of the herd. He loved the feel of the wind against his face. The way the world flew by in streams of colour. He pranced and galloped. For the first time in his life, Ross felt fully free. And alive!

Ross, still in his Fire Steed skin, visited Bernard on the night of their fourth day at the Skinwalker camp.

"There's something I'm never going to get used to." Bernard stared with wide eyes. "I can hardly believe it."

"Yet, here I am." Ross's happiness dimmed at the sight of his best friend tied and bound. "I'm going to talk to Seb in the morning. We need to go after the ring before Lord Damon can organize his army. If we let that happen, Lord Damon will kill every One-Skin in his way." Ross blushed when he realized what he'd said. "I mean 'human.' If we're going after Lord Damon, I want you with me."

"What about me?" Cat had crept in without them hearing. She put her hand on Ross's broad, muscled back. "You're right to want Bernard along. But Seb may not see things the way you do."

"Leave that to me." Ross stomped his front hoof. "I'll make him see."

Cat leaned on Ross. She took Bernard's hand in hers. "We'll do it together," she promised.

CHAPTER TWELVE | Plan of Attack

Ross and Catherine talked with Seb throughout the morning of the fifth day. Finally, the old man agreed to set Bernard free. "But you will answer for his actions," Seb warned Ross. "This is the only way our people will accept my decision."

"Bernard is an honorable friend." Ross stood firm. "I'd stake my life on it."

"Let us hope it never comes to that." Seb turned to the sentries. "Release the One-Skin and bring him to me. He will join us in our quest for the ring."

The pig-like man with tusks snorted, "Working with One-Skins! What's next, sleeping with the wolves?" He stomped off angrily to fetch Bernard.

As the day's light faded, the leaders of the Skinwalker clans gathered around a crackling fire. Seb had called a meeting to organize their plan to take back the ring from Lord Damon. Some came in their animal skins. Some leaned against trees or sat near the fire in their human skins. Others, like the man with tusks, walked upright but kept a piece of their animal-self visible.

Ross asked Cat why that was.

"Some things are just easier to do with hands," she explained. "Like drawing a sword or bow. But many, like Hugo there, are fiercely proud of their animal clans. They never fully change into human form unless it's necessary. Besides," Cat lowered her voice so only Ross could hear, "he's proud of those tusks of his and shows them off whenever he can."

"Ah," Ross looked over to the man with tusks. "So that grumpy little fellow is named Hugo. Is he a boar?"

Cat's laugh came out like a roar. "In more ways than one." She sobered and looked around the fire. "As for me, I prefer this skin when I need to show strength. Let's face it, nobody's going to argue with me once I show them my teeth and claws." She pulled back her upper lip and flexed her paws.

Ross gulped at the sight. He was glad she was on his side for the upcoming battle. He was about to say more, but Seb motioned for silence.

On through the night they planned their attack. It would all begin at dawn.

~

The sun had been up for two hours when Ross reached the bridge at the east entrance to Lord Damon's castle. Their boots made a thumping sound as they crossed the wooden bridge. Cat's panther paws tread without a sound. Both Ross and Bernard's hands were tied in front of them. Cat had the other end of the rope in her mouth. She led them to the castle gate.

Ross worked through the plan in his head. His group had their numbers and the element of surprise in their favor. They'd planned their attack at a time of day when the sun would be in the east. Seb's group of Skinwalker warriors would have the sun at their backs as they attacked. Lord Damon's wolves would have it in their eyes. The only problem was finding a way through the solid iron gate of Lord Damon's castle. That's where Cat came in.

"Hurry along, you vermin," she growled around the rope. She gave the rope a tug and Ross stumbled forward. "Lord Damon will be pleased to see these two," Cat called to the guard on duty. "Open the gate."

Ross thought about Seb and the others who were hiding in the long grass. He tested the air with his nose. Good. The wind was coming from the west. The wolf guards wouldn't catch their scent until it was too late. Sweat formed on Ross's forehead and under his arms. Would this work?

Then the gate groaned open.

Ross took in his surroundings. He tapped into his keen senses of smell and sound. Ross could smell only the scents of the Skinwalkers. All the One-Skins who had once lived there were already dead.

Up ahead, they heard footsteps and armor. A guard in his wolf skin scratched and yawned. There were five, maybe six guards at the entrance.

"Took you long enough to find 'em," one guard said. "Lord Damon's not very patient, you know."

"It took a while to catch them. This one runs faster than you'd think." Cat turned to wink at Ross. "And speaking of that, I'd better check these ropes." Cat turned. With one quick bite from her razor teeth, she cut the ropes around Ross's hands. Then she cut Bernard's.

Cat roared and sent the signal to the others hiding outside. Then she cut down the first guard with one swipe of her paw. With lightning speed, she leapt after the others.

Ross and Bernard raced to the castle gates and threw them open wide.

Skinwalkers charged from the field in a wave of fur, claw and muscle. Each chose the form that served them best in combat. Bears bellowed as they ran. Elk in their human skins wielded swords and bows. Hugo grunted around his tusks. He clutched a huge axe in his thick fist as he led his clan forward. Feet thumped. The air filled with the sound of the coming battle.

The ground shook as the Skinwalkers crossed the bridge and flooded through the gates.

A bell clanged in a tower overhead. Intruders! Wolves poured from the castle and into the courtyard. They growled and bared their teeth.

Ross and Bernard took swords from the fallen guards and fought their way through the courtyard.

Hugo swung his axe and grunted. "Charge!" he called out and used his head like a battering ram. As he came within reach of the castle doors, four wolves cornered Hugo. "Squeal, little pig," one taunted him. Then they attacked.

Bernard, with a sword in each hand, jumped into the fight. He cut down two wolves while Hugo defeated the others.

"I was doing fine on my own," Hugo grunted.

"You're welcome," Bernard called over his shoulder. Then he ran to the small dark corner where Ross and Cat waited.

Ross watched the chaos around him with wide eyes. Flesh and fur fought wildly. Bodies lay bleeding on the ground. The air was filled with screams, howls and shouts.

"It's time," Cat whispered.

Because of the noise and madness of battle, no one saw Cat, Ross and Bernard slip into the shadows. The three of them stole quietly through the servants' door into the castle.

CHAPTER THIRTEEN | Surprise

Soon Cat, Ross and Bernard reached the hall that led to the castle's main chamber. Two huge doors stood open. From inside, Ross could hear Lord Damon's voice barking orders. He signaled for Bernard to take cover behind one of the doors. Ross hid behind the other. Now! Ross motioned to Cat.

She hurried into the room. "Lord Damon!" she called. "They're attacking everywhere. I tried to fight them off, but there are too many. We must get you to safety."

Ross wished he could see their faces. Did they believe Cat? Would their plan work?

The sound of the battle in the courtyard rang through the air. Something crashed against the main entrance doors.

"Quickly, my lord," Cat shouted. "If they manage to break through, there won't be time. We must leave now." Cat let loose a deafening roar.

Cat's panther feet tread into the hall. "Now, my lord," she called. "The way is clear."

Two wolves growled as they followed after her. "The She-cat speaks true, Lord. Follow us."

"Let's be done with it, then." Lord Damon said as he left the chamber. Ross heard two other wolves behind him. "The rest of you," Lord Damon called into the room. "Go out into the courtyard. Bring those beasts down."

The air filled with yips and yowls. Dozens of wolves ran through the halls and out into the noisy fray.

Ross pressed his back against the wall. Fear hung in the air like a black cloud. He could smell it in the sweat from the wolves' bodies. Ross's heart beat wildly in his chest. How could no one hear its steady thump, thump, thump? He tightened his grip on the swords he held in each hand.

As the sound of footsteps grew faint, Ross heard Cat speak in the distance. "Not to worry, Lord Damon, we have you now."

It was their signal to follow. Ross tapped lightly on the other chamber door.

"Four guards and Lord Damon. At least we're evenly matched," Bernard whispered as he stepped from behind the door.

"We won't be for long once the rest realize what

we're up to." Ross thumped Bernard's shoulder. "Let's be quick about it."

Ross and Bernard tiptoed through the east hall. The plan was for Cat to lead Lord Damon the same way they'd come in. Then they'd go down the south hall and out the servants' entrance.

When they reached the point where the east hall turned to go south, Ross raised his hand. "Wait," he whispered. He quickly stole a look around the corner. "They're about half-way there. We're not going to get a better chance than now." Ross raised three fingers.

One. Two. Three.

Ross gripped his swords and raced into the hall. Bernard followed close behind. Lord Damon and his guards turned at the sound of their battle cry.

Cat had been in the lead. She turned as the others faced their attackers. That was how they'd planned it. Ross and Bernard attacking from the north. Cat from the south. Lord Damon and his four guards were trapped between them.

"Hurry, She-cat. Protect Lord Damon," one of the guards ordered.

Cat bared her teeth in a deadly smile. "Surprise." Then she flicked the guard aside with her paw.

Ross's heart raced as he sped down the hallway. He

lowered his blades to proper thrusting height. Ross, Bernard and Cat were slowly closing in on Lord Damon. He was trapped.

But Lord Damon didn't seem worried. A wide smile spread across his face. Then he started to clap his hands slowly. Ross's mother's ring shone in the lantern's light.

"Well done, young man," Lord Damon said to him. "You got farther than I'd thought you would. But did you really think it would be that easy? I am the only one worthy of wearing this ring!" Lord Damon raised his fist to the ceiling and let out a loud howl.

The doors to the chambers along the hallway burst open. Through them poured dozens of wolves.

"Foolish boy. Surely, you didn't think I'd send my entire royal guard into battle and leave myself with only four guards to protect me." Lord Damon motioned for the wolves to attack.

Now Ross, Bernard and Cat were the ones trapped. Wolves surrounded them on every side. They growled and bared their teeth.

"So much for being evenly matched." Bernard swung his swords as he spoke. "What do we do now?"

Ross gripped his swords tighter. "Now we fight!"

Swords clanked and fur flew as Ross and Bernard cut down each wolf as it pounced. Cat sunk her teeth into the throat of one wolf. Her knife-like claws sliced through another. But she let out a cry when a third wolf jumped her from behind. The wolf landed on her back and dug its teeth into her shoulder. She reached back and grabbed it in her jaws. Then she shook the life from it.

Ross continued to thrust with his swords. Wolves yipped and howled in pain. Some lay bleeding or dead on the floor, others backed away. Ross's shoulders and arms ached from his swinging blows. But still he fought.

Ross and Bernard had cut their numbers to half when the wolves changed tactics. Ross watched in horror as five wolves turned on Bernard. All five attacked at once.

"No!" Ross's voice boomed. He watched as Bernard fought wildly, his two swords flying.

"You hadn't planned on that, had you, boy?" Lord Damon taunted.

Ross felt his blood boil. "And you hadn't planned on this!" Ross's tunic ripped as he changed skin. It fell in shreds at his hoofed feet.

"How? When?" Lord Damon sputtered.

But Ross was already running to Bernard's aid. Ross stomped down hard with his front hooves. The first wolf's spine broke beneath them. Ross — as a Fire Stallion — kicked and bit, tossing wolves against the wall as if they were made of rags.

"Bernard?" Ross cried. He leaned over his friend's body as it lay in a heap on the floor. Blood oozed from Bernard's left shoulder. His arm lay at an odd angle to his body.

"I'm fine," Bernard said through his pain. "Never mind me. Help Cat."

Ross turned to see Cat fighting against terrible odds. Wolves attacked her from all sides. She yowled as they dug their teeth into her. For every one she cut down, two more came.

Ross tossed his head high and snorted. He charged. Wolves yelped, then wheezed their last breath.

Side by side, Ross and Cat fought.

Still more wolves came.

A corner of Ross's mind heard the crash of timbers in the distance. There were loud shouts. The stomping of many feet on flagstone. Wolves yipped and yelped. Someone yelled out, "Retreat!"

Skinwalkers poured into the castle halls. The air was filled with the sounds of them pushing forward. Hugo was the first to barrel down the south hall. He rammed his tusks into a wolf's belly and sent it flying. "Thought you might need some help," he called.

More Skinwalkers followed.

Ross pulled in ragged breaths. His lungs felt like they were on fire. His heart beat so fast he thought it would explode. Ross kicked as a wolf attacked his forelegs.

We're winning! thought Ross. Wolves retreated in all directions.

Hugo raised his axe high and bellowed, "Victory!"

Then a movement caught the corner of Ross's eye. He turned to see Lord Damon slipping out the servants' door.

CHAPTER FOURTEEN
A Different Kind of War

Hugo followed Ross's gaze. "That coward. Damon is slinking away like a snake in the grass." Hugo shook his axe. "Let's be after him, then," he urged Ross.

Ross shook his long red mane. "I'll go after him. It is my right, after all." He turned to Hugo. "Help Cat get to the dungeons. Her brother is still down there, and there may still be some guards. Will you do that for me?"

Hugo smiled and bowed low. "After today, I'd pledge my life and my axe to your service. Now hurry. The ring should be yours, young King. You must get it back."

Ross headed to the door, then stopped. "I think Bernard's arm is broken. See he gets help too!" he called out to Hugo.

Ross was out the door before Hugo could reply.

The sun was now high in the afternoon sky. It left long shadows along the courtyard. There were many places for a wolf or a man to hide. Ross tested the air with his nose. He twitched his ears and listened. All he heard was the muffled sounds of the waning battle within the castle walls.

Ross looked around the corner to the north where the courtyard led to the main bridge. He shook his head. There were too many Skinwalkers at that entrance. Lord Damon would not risk it. Then Ross looked to the west. That way led only into dark shadows cast by the castle walls. He nodded his head and set off into the darkness.

Around him was a strange contrast. The silence in the shadowy courtyard. The sounds of fighting from inside the castle walls. It made the hair on Ross's back stand up. He drew back his ears and moved farther into the long narrow courtyard.

Ahead, Ross saw the outline of hay bales propped against the castle wall. They stood easily twice his height. As he got closer, he saw something black lying on the ground in front of them. It was a cloak. Lord

Damon's cloak.

He must have changed into his wolf skin, Ross thought. *But where is he?*

He tested the air again. The wind had changed direction now. Ross wouldn't be able to catch Lord Damon's scent. But Lord Damon could catch his!

Ross looked to the tall bales of hay against the castle wall to his right. The great stone fence around the courtyard was to his left. It turned when the courtyard came to an abrupt stop twenty feet ahead.

Filth and maggots, cursed Ross. *I've walked into a trap.*

Ross considered what to do. He had two choices: flee or fight. He shook his red mane and stomped his front hooves. "Lord Damon!" Ross called out. "Stop hiding in the shadows. Face me!"

"My pleasure," said Lord Damon's voice from above.

Ross quickly looked up. But he was too late.

Lord Damon leapt from the top of the hay bales. His white ears were drawn back. His sharp teeth were bared. His eyes were red with fury.

Ross cried out as Lord Damon's claws dug into his back and shoulders. White hot pain shot through him as Lord Damon sank his teeth into Ross's neck. A few inches lower and the bite would have killed him. Ross knew he had to act quickly before Lord Damon's razor

teeth found their mark.

Ross bucked with all his might. He kicked frantically with his back hooves. Sparks ignited beneath them. The hay began to smolder. Then it began to burn.

The hay was on fire!

Lord Damon yelped as he suddenly lost grip with his hind paws. He slipped sideways and dug his front claws more deeply into Ross's back and shoulders.

Ross used the advantage to lean his head back. He sank his teeth into Lord Damon's pelt and pulled with all his might.

Lord Damon howled as he flew from Ross's back. Then he landed with a thump onto the straw covered ground.

The fire that began in the hay bales spread quickly. It licked against the castle wall and snaked across the ground. Then the straw beneath Lord Damon caught fire. Lord Damon's eyes grew wide. He cowered in fear, then backed slowly until he was stopped by the castle fence's north wall. There was nowhere else to run.

"Where is the ring?" Ross shouted over the growing flames.

Lord Damon yelped and backed farther into a corner. "If you let me die, the ring dies with me," he called.

But the ring was not about to disappear. There it was,

hooked around Lord Damon's back tooth. The gold reflected the fire's light.

The fire burned brightly. It formed a wall of flame that separated Ross from Lord Damon. Ross judged the height and distance. Could he do it?

Ross backed up, then sped forward at a full gallop. He jumped high into the air. The flames barely missed his belly.

With his teeth, Ross lifted Lord Damon by the scruff of his neck. He tossed him quickly past the wall of flames. Then Ross leapt with all the might of a Fire-Stallion. He landed a few feet from where Lord Damon lay panting and beaten.

There was a part of Ross that wanted to finish this. All he had to do was stomp down hard on Lord Damon's spine. The bones would splinter and Lord Damon would live no more. The thoughts raced through his mind as Ross waged a different kind of war. A war of conscience.

Ross placed his hoof against Lord Damon's throat to keep him from moving. Then he made his decision.

"Skinwalkers!" he called to those who were starting to fill the courtyard. "Bring some chains to bind Lord Damon. There's been enough blood shed this day."

The battle was won.

Ross felt exhausted and excited all at the same time.

He accepted Hugo's offer of a clean tunic so that he could change skins.

Carefully, Ross cradled his mother's ring in his hand. Then he slipped it on his finger. On his hand was the ring of a Skinwalker King.

Ross watched the Skinwalkers bring water and put out the courtyard fire. Lord Damon was taken away in chains. Then Ross looked up to see Cat emerge from the castle. She too had changed skins. Her long black hair flew in the breeze. Leaning against her was her brother.

In all his days, Ross would never forget the smile she gave him.

CHAPTER FIFTEEN
Hail to the New King!

That night, the Skinwalker camp rang with noise and music. Ross stood in the fire's glow and let its flames warm him. His mother's ring — the ring of a Skinwalker king — rested on the third finger of his left hand. Ross touched it again. He still found it hard to believe that it was there.

"It is good to see the ring where it belongs." Old Seb crossed his arm in front of his waist and bowed low. "You have the makings of a fine young king."

"I don't feel much like a king," Ross confessed. "To be

honest, I'm not sure that I'd even know what to do as king."

Seb stood tall and looked at Ross with kind eyes. "Anyone can be born into royalty. However, a true king must learn to rule. You, my son, have a good soul and a wise heart. There are many here who can guide and help you."

Ross stared into the fire. It all seemed so big, so . . . impossible. Yet here he was.

Ross followed Seb into the crowd of Skinwalkers. They parted like a wave as Ross approached. Many bowed low to the ground as he passed.

Ross found Bernard, with his arm in a sling, sitting beneath a tree. His other hand held a tankard of ale. "Carrot Head!" Bernard shouted. "Come. Drink!"

Ross laughed at the familiar joke. He would have to keep Bernard with him. Bernard would make sure that Ross stayed humble. Then Ross noticed that Bernard sat alone — away from the crowd.

"Why are you sitting here by yourself?" Ross accepted Bernard's offer of some ale. He took a long sip.

"I'm a One-Skin, remember. Not all your friends are happy to have me here."

Ross looked around to see some Skinwalkers whispering and pointing. They stopped as they saw his gaze turn angry. "That's silly," he told Bernard. "You fought bravely today. I wouldn't have made it to Lord Damon and the ring without you."

"Don't get tied up in a knot over it." Bernard took another gulp of ale. "You can't change years of distrust and anger in just a day." Then Bernard gave Ross a friendly punch with his good arm. "Besides, it seems to me that you're in a position to change that if you've got a mind to."

"I will do what I can," Ross replied.

Bernard nodded, then changed the subject. "Have you seen Cat?"

Ross had seen her. She too sat away from the crowd. She tended her brother who was still weak from being in prison. Ross clicked Bernard's cup with his and then headed to where Cat sat.

"You're quiet tonight." Ross took a seat in the grass beside her. "You've had a grand day. First the battle and now you're back here with your brother. Why aren't you having fun?"

"Haven't you seen how they treat Bernard?" Cat replied. "After all he's done for us! Why can't they understand? In any clan, Skinwalker or One-Skin, there is good and bad."

Ross put his hand over hers. He looked into her eyes

and swallowed hard. "Perhaps it's time to make them understand."

Ross moved to the center of the camp. He motioned for Bernard to join him. Then Ross raised his cup high. "A toast! To the bravest One-Skin and finest friend I've ever known." Then he drank deeply.

A sudden silence fell over the camp. Skinwalkers exchanged whispers and glances. Ross watched them but still held his cup high.

"A toast!" Old Seb chimed in. "To Bernard!"

Hugo barreled forward and raised his axe. "And to one of the bravest One-Skins I've had the pleasure of knowing!" Then Hugo drank his ale dry.

Some joined in. Others kept their cups stubbornly low.

Ross stood before them. "A friend told me that you cannot change years of distrust and anger in one day. But I am here to tell you that we must change. Good and evil do not belong to any one clan: Skinwalker or One-Skin. They lie in the choices we make. In the way we treat each other.

"King Rudgerd is an evil man. He kills our brothers and sisters without mercy. But this King is not like all One-Skins. There are many good and kind humans among them. I have lived with them. I know this to be true."

Ross raised his left fist high. His ring shone in the firelight. "I stand before you tonight after a great victory. But there is another battle to be won. A battle for all that is right. We must not let the history of war and distrust dictate our future. Together we can build our world, Skinwalker and One-Skins, a world where all may live in peace."

Many stood now and raised their cups.

"To the future!" Ross called.

"To the future!" they answered.

Ross looked around at all the hopeful faces. He nodded and smiled.

It was a beginning.

The year is 1144 and the world's last dragon has returned. The evil Lord Manning plans to use that dragon to rule the kingdom. According to prophecy, only one person can stop him. And that one person is a sixteen-year-old boy.

BOOK 1: *The Last Dragon* Jacob, Orson and Lia must rescue the only egg of the world's last dragon.

BOOK 2: *A Hero's Worth* While the young dragon grows, Lia may be forced to marry Lord Manning.

BOOK 3: *Draco's Fire* The fully grown dragon helps Jacob fulfill the prophecy — and rescue his kingdom.

About the Author

D.M. Ouellet is an accomplished author of poetry and children's stories but has always loved fantasy. Her first fantasy novel for High Interest Publishing was *A Hero's Worth* in the Dragon Speaker series. Her recent children's book *How Robin Saved Spring* (illustrated by Nicoletta Ceccoli) is a best seller. Visit her website at www.debbieouellet.com for more information about all her writing.

For more information on HIP novels:
High Interest Publishing
www.hip-books.com